"See You Later, Mashed Potater!"

By Anna H. Dickson
Illustrated by Tom Brannon

A SESAME STREET/GOLDEN PRESS BOOK

Published by Western Publishing Company, Inc., in conjunction with Children's Television Workshop.

"Where are you going, Snuffy?" asked Baby Alice Snuffleupagus.

"I'm going to school. You get to stay home and have the snuffle blocks all to yourself! You can build me a castle. I'll come home right after school.

"See you later, Alligator!" said Snuffy, waving good-bye.

"I'm not an alligator. I'm a Snuffleupagus!" Alice called after him.

The snuffle cave seemed quiet without a big brother
Snuffleupagus lumbering around.

"Do you want to start that castle now?" asked
Mommy Snuffle. "Or would you like some tomato
juice?"

"I think I will drink my juice while I build a castle,"
sniffed Alice.

She used all the snuffle blocks for the castle.

Then Alice went out to the garden with Granny and dug up carrots for a while.

"Would you like to go to the arbor and swing?" asked Granny Snuffle when Alice brought her the carrots.

"I like Snuffy to push me," said Alice.

"Maybe later, Elevator!" said Granny.

Snuffy brought his friend Big Bird home with him from school. They found Alice tying a ribbon in Delilah's hair.

"Hello, Alice!" said Snuffy. "I came home just like I said I would. And Big Bird came, too!"

Snuffy, Big Bird, and Alice went out to play on the swing. Snuffy and Big Bird took turns pushing Alice. Then they all took turns swinging. They swang and swang until it was time for dinner.

"Where are you going, Big Bird?" asked Alice when Big Bird hoisted his bookbag on his shoulder.

"I have to go home now, Alice," he said. "It's almost dinnertime."

"Oh, no. Don't go, Bird!" said Baby Alice.

"I'll come back another time and we'll swing again," said Big Bird.

"So good-bye, Pumpkin Pie!"

"I'm not a pumpkin pie," called Alice. "I'm a Snuffleupagus!"

After dinner Mommy and Daddy Snuffle put on their hats and coats.

"Where are you going?" asked Alice.

"We're going to our Block Association meeting, Dear," said Mommy. "Granny is going to stay with you. And we won't be out late."

"It's time for you to go to bed anyway," said Daddy. "I'll tuck you in."

"I don't want you to go to a meeting, Daddy," said Alice. "I want you to read me a story."

"Your brother will tell you a bedtime story," said Daddy. "Sleep well, Stinkerbell."

"I'm not a Stinkerbell," said Alice. "I'm a Snuffleupagus!"

"So don't wait up for us, Snuffleupagus."

When Mommy and Daddy came home that night, the snuffle cave was still and quiet. Granny Snuffle was dozing in her rocking chair. Snuffy was snoring on the sofa.

Mommy and Daddy tucked Snuffy into his own bed and kissed him good night.

Alice was sound asleep in her snuggy bed upstairs.
Mommy and Daddy shuffled silently into her room and
gave her snuffle kisses.

"We're home," they whispered. "Good night."

On Sunday Granny asked Alice to help shut her suitcase.

"Where are you going, Granny?" asked Alice.

"It's time for me to go back home, Dear. Remember when I told you about your Snuffle cousins coming to visit me? Well, I have to go home and make cole slaw and spaghetti soup for them."

"I don't want you to go home, Granny," said Alice. And a little snuffle tear shone on her fuzzy cheek. "I want you to stay and rock me and sing me snuffle songs like you do."

Granny Snuffle sat Alice in her lap. They rocked and sang "Snuffle Off to Buffalo" together. They were just finishing "Let a Snuffle Be Your Umbrella" when a taxi honked outside.

"That's my ride to the airport," said Granny.

"Now, you practice our songs while I'm gone, Alice!" said Granny. "Don't forget. And when I come back for the holidays, we'll sing them for the whole Snuffle family."

"Sniff," answered Alice.

Granny gave every member of the Snuffleupagus family a hug and a kiss. She hugged and kissed Alice last.

"Granny," said Alice, "you forgot your beautiful shawl."

"My goodness," said Granny. "I can't get one more thing in my suitcase. Alice, will you please take care of my shawl for me? I'll need it when I come back."

Granny wrapped her beautiful shawl around Alice's shoulders.

Granny got into the taxi with her suitcase.
"See you later, Mashed Potater!" she called to Alice
as she rode away.

The next day Big Bird came over again after school. Big Bird, Snuffy, and Alice were playing snuffle-ball in the yard when Mommy Snuffleupagus came outside and called to Alice.

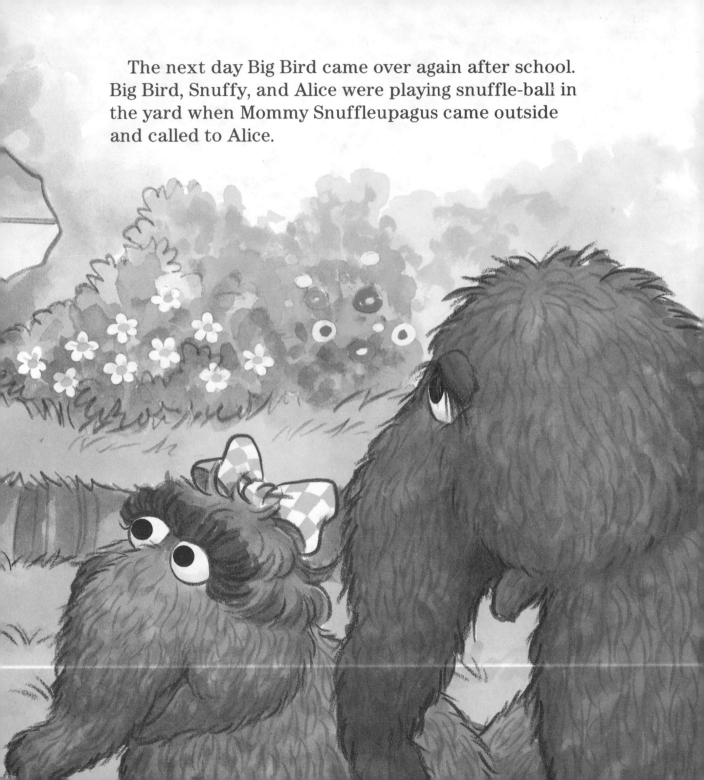

"Elmo's mommy just called," said Mommy Snuffle. "Elmo wants you to come over to play. His mommy has invited you to stay for dinner and spend the night. Would you like to do that?"

"May I take Delilah?" asked Alice.

"Yes, Dear. But you don't have to stay if you don't want to."

"Yes, yes, I want to!" cried Alice. "And Delilah wants to stay, too!"

Alice packed her little suitcase with all the
important things she would need overnight at Elmo's,
and closed it tight.

"Where are you going?" asked Snuffy and Big Bird.

"I'm going to eat dinner at Elmo's house and spend
the night," answered Alice.

"You are?" asked Snuffy.

"You are?" asked Big Bird.

Alice was all ready to go when Elmo and his mommy
came to pick her up at the Snuffle cave.

Alice kissed Mommy good-bye. "I'll be home in the
morning, Mommy.

"We can finish our snuffle-ball game tomorrow, Bird.

"You may have my dessert, Snuffy.

"See you later, 'Frigerator!" said Alice, waving good-bye.